Mini Sweets

Candy Fairies

Mini Sweets

HELEN PERELMAN

ILLUSTRATED BY
ERICA-JANE WATERS

ALADDIN
NEW YORK LONDON TORONTO SYDNEY NEW DELHI

ALADDIN

An imprint of Simon & Schuster Children's Publishing Division

1230 Avenue of the Americas, New York, New York 10020

First Aladdin hardcover edition January 2017

Text copyright © 2017 by Helen Perelman

Illustrations copyright © 2017 by Erica-Jane Waters

Also available in an Aladdin paperback edition.

All rights reserved, including the right of reproduction in whole or in part in any form.

ALADDIN and related logo are registered trademarks of Simon & Schuster, Inc.

For information about special discounts for bulk purchases, please contact Simon & Schuster Special Sales at 1-866-506-1949 or business@simonandschuster.com.

The Simon & Schuster Speakers Bureau can bring authors to your live event. For more information or to book an event contact the Simon & Schuster Speakers Bureau at 1-866-248-3049 or visit our website at www.simonspeakers.com.

Jacket designed by Karina Granda

Interior designed by Nina Simoneaux

The text of this book was set in Baskerville Book.

Manufactured in the United States of America 1216 FFG

2 4 6 8 10 9 7 5 3 1

Library of Congress Control Number 2016953370

ISBN 978-1-4814-4684-6 (hc)

ISBN 978-1-4814-4683-9 (pbk)

ISBN 978-1-4814-4685-3 (eBook)

For all the Candy Fairies fans!

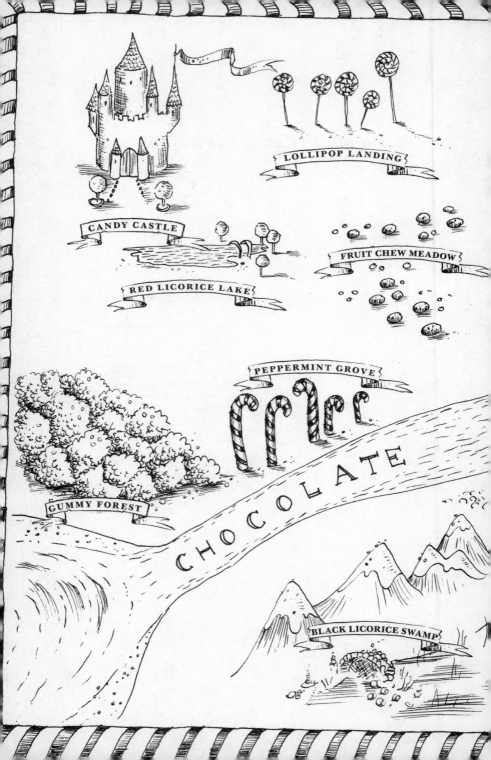

Contents

CHAPTER
1

Sweet Sun Dip

Berry the Fruit Fairy flew across Sugar Valley. She had been in the Sour Orchard picking fruit gems for her latest dress design and hadn't realized how late it had gotten! Sometimes Berry got caught up in her fashion designs and lost track of time. The sun was sliding quickly toward the top of the Frosted

Mountains. Soon it would be Sun Dip, the time of day when Berry and her Candy Fairy friends got together at Licorice Lake to watch the sunset. They liked to catch up with one another and eat sweet treats.

"There you are!" Melli the Caramel Fairy exclaimed as Berry landed on the red sugar sand at the lake.

"I was getting worried!" Raina the Gummy Fairy said.

Berry smiled. "I wouldn't miss Sun Dip and Melli's fresh caramels," she said. "And I want to see Princess Dash." A smile spread across her face. "I'm still not used to saying that," she said, giggling.

Their friend Dash the Mint Fairy had been crowned Peppermint Princess when it was

discovered she was from a line of Mint royalty in Peppermint Kingdom. Dash's great-great-grandparents were king and queen of the frozen Peppermint Kingdom on Ice Cream Isles. Long ago, when an evil ogre threatened their palace and candy, the royals moved to Peppermint Grove in Sugar Valley for safety. Now Dash split her time between Candy Kingdom and the Ice Cream Isles. She tried to get back for a few Sun Dips each month. Berry loved seeing her Mint Fairy friend and hearing all about princess life in the frozen Peppermint Kingdom.

"Hello!" Dash called to Berry. She flew to her friend and gave her a tight squeeze. She peered over Berry's shoulder to get a look into Melli's basket. "And Melli made my favorite caramels! What an extra-sweet Sun Dip!"

Melli lifted up the basket. "Yes," she said. "Fresh caramel for the princess."

"Oh, stop calling me princess," Dash said. She sat down on the blanket. "But I will take a caramel candy!"

"But you *are* a princess," Melli told her.

"I'm still Dash the Mint Fairy, and your friend." Dash stood tall and stuck out her chest proudly.

Berry laughed. "That's for sure," she said. She sat next to Dash and opened her bag. "Wait till you see the *sugar-tastic* gems I found in Sour Orchard today."

Dash rolled her eyes. The sporty Mint Fairy was not so enthusiastic about sugar gems. Even though Dash was now a princess, she was still the same minty sports-loving Candy Fairy she had always been.

"Dash, even you will be impressed," Berry said. She unwrapped her package with care. "These gems will make any outfit shine for Mini's ball!"

The royal ball was the talk of Sugar Valley. It was a grand party for Princess Lolli and Prince Scoop's baby, Princess Mini, to celebrate her first birthday. The whole kingdom was preparing for the event.

"You were getting gems for your outfit?" Cocoa the Chocolate Fairy asked.

"My outfit *and* all of your outfits too," Berry replied with a wink. "This is going to be a delicious party. There will be fairies from all the kingdoms there. Everyone wants to celebrate Princess Mini's first birthday. And we are all going to look *sugar-tastic*!"

"I'm more interested in the sugar bowl touch," Dash said. "When the sugar bowl is put in front of Princess Mini, I want to see what kind of candy she makes with her touch."

"Everyone in Sugar Valley is waiting to see what her talent will be," Raina said. At a Candy Fairy's first birthday, a sugar bowl was placed in front of the baby. When the baby fairy touched the sugar, a candy would appear, and at that moment everyone would know what type of Candy Fairy the young fairy would become. For a royal baby, the sugar bowl touch was a much bigger occasion.

"Candy Fairy or Ice Cream Fairy?" Raina asked. "What do you think?"

Dash popped a mint chocolate in her mouth. "I have no idea!" She licked her fingers. "But she is a supersweet baby fairy princess."

The five Candy Fairies loved being with Princess Mini. Because they were so close with Princess Lolli and Prince Scoop, they had already spent a lot of time with the little princess.

"I hope she is a Candy Fairy," Berry said.

"Me too," Melli said. "But being an Ice Cream Fairy like her dad would be pretty sweet."

Cocoa nodded. "That is true," she said. "But she could be like her aunt Princess Sprinkle and make cupcakes and cakes."

Dash laughed. "No matter what, sure as sugar, she is the *sweetest*!"

"We can agree on that," Raina said. "And this ball is going to be *sweet-tacular*! Berry, let's see your drawings of the dresses."

Berry rolled out her dress drawings on Melli's blanket. She showed her friends the new styles she was creating for the royal ball. "See the space on the collar? That is where I am going to put these sugar gems," she told her friends.

"*Sugar-tastic!*" Raina exclaimed. She reached for a bright red cherry gummy flower that was sticking out of Berry's bag. "This is beautiful," she said. "What's the gummy flower for?"

"I picked this fruit flower to give to Princess Mini when we see her next," Berry said. "Remember, we grew these in Fruit Chew Meadow?"

Raina clapped her hands. "I do!" she said. "Mini will love that."

A sugar fly buzzed by Dash's face and dropped a note in her hand. "Oh, look," Dash said. "It's a note from Princess Lolli and Prince Scoop!"

"Read it to us," Cocoa told Dash.

"The letter says," Dash said, unfolding the note, "'Please come to tea tomorrow at Candy

Castle, with love, Princess Lolli and Prince Scoop.' We're going, sure as sugar!" She wrote a reply back and sent the sugar fly on its way.

Raina tapped her chin with her finger. "Hmm, I wonder what they want to ask us."

"What makes you think they want to ask us something?" Dash said. She reached over for another one of Melli's caramels. "These are so good, Melli!"

"Thanks, Dash," Melli said. "It's a new candy I am trying out."

"I bet this invitation has something to do with the Mini Ball," Berry said.

"Maybe," Cocoa replied. "This is going to be one huge celebration for all of Sugar Valley."

"And we're going to look sparkly and delicious," Berry added. She rolled up her dress drawings. "I am going to make sure of that."

"No matter what," Raina said, "this is going to be a happy celebration for the delicious royal baby."

"That is the sugar-honest truth," Berry said, grinning. She gathered up her new gems and put them safely in her bag. She couldn't wait to get started on designing the dresses for the royal ball.

CHAPTER

2

Fairysitters

Tea at Candy Castle was a grand event. The gold and rainbow royal teacups were set out on an extra-long dining table with trays of fancy candies from all over Sugar Valley. The five Candy Fairies were sitting on the edge of their seats as they waited for the royal family to join them.

"Everything looks almost too pretty to eat!" Raina exclaimed. "Look at those chocolates and caramels!"

"Don't be shy," Dash said, reaching for a treat from the nearest tray. "Teatime is about eating the sweets!"

"And about having good manners," Berry added. "We should wait for Princess Lolli and Prince Scoop before we eat."

"Why do you think Princess Lolli asked us here today?" Cocoa said. She kept her eye on the door.

Dash licked her fingers. "I don't know," she said. "But I love tea at the castle."

"Oh, Dash," Berry said, laughing. "You just love sweet treats."

Princess Lolli flew into the room with Princess Mini in her arms and Prince Scoop by her side. "Hello," she said as she entered.

The five friends gathered around Princess Lolli. They wanted to take a peek at the baby. Princess Mini was fast asleep in a bundle of pink cotton candy blankets.

"She looks scrumptious!" Berry exclaimed. "And much bigger than last week when we saw her." Mini's strawberry blonde hair was just like Princess Lolli's and her eyes were the same color as Prince Scoop's. She was the perfect blend of both her parents.

"She's growing fast," Prince Scoop said. "She's even saying a few words now."

Berry wanted Mini to wake up from her nap. She wanted to give her the gummy flower and hear her new words.

"Come sit down and have something to eat," Princess Lolli said. "I'm going to let Mini sleep." She placed the baby in a crib in the corner of the room.

Prince Scoop sat next to Dash. He pushed a plate toward her. "Try the chocolate mint squares," he said with a wink. "They were just delivered this morning."

"Yum," Dash said, taking one. "Thank you!"

"We're so happy to have you all here," Prince Scoop said, looking around the table. "We've asked you here because we need a favor."

Berry jumped up. "We're happy to help!" she exclaimed.

Princess Lolli smiled. "Thank you," she said. "Prince Scoop and I are counting on your help." She nodded to the sleeping princess. "We need to go to Cake Kingdom for three days and we'd like you to stay here at the castle and be fairysitters while we are gone."

"A castle sleepover?" Melli asked. She dropped her chocolate-covered strawberry on her plate.

"Yes," Princess Lolli told her. "The Castle Fairies will help out, but Mini knows you all the best and loves being with you. It would make us feel better knowing you were here to look after her and play with her. Would you do it?"

"Sure as sugar!" Raina said, answering for all her friends.

Dash giggled. "A royal sleepover!"

"Sweet strawberries," Berry said. "That sounds perfect."

Just then Princess Mini began to cry. Berry was the first one to her crib. "Look what I have, Mini," she said. From her bag Berry took out the cherry-red gummy flower she had showed her friends at Sun Dip. The bright red got Mini's attention and she stopped crying. She reached for the flower and started giggling. "Gummy!" Mini said.

"You see," Princess Lolli said. "I feel much better with you all staying here with Mini."

Berry returned to her seat. "I'm glad she likes the flower. Raina and I planted those together," she said.

Prince Scoop picked up Mini and brought her to the table. "I'd say she loves it," he said.

"Thank you." He snuggled his daughter. "The whole kingdom is talking about you, Mini." He looked up at the Candy Fairies. "What's your guess about her sugar talent?"

Raina pulled out a copy of the *Daily Scoop*

from her bag. "There is a whole page here about Princess Mini and the sugar bowl," she said. She lifted up the paper. "Everyone wants to know, including us!"

Princess Lolli sighed. "I know this is important to everyone, but I think there is too much attention on what her talent will be," she said. She flew to Princess Mini and touched her forehead. "Whatever

Mini's talent is will be supersweet and we will be very proud."

"We *all* will be," Raina added.

"We have another favor to ask of you," Prince Scoop said. He looked over at Princess Lolli. "Can you five get the sugar for the sugar bowl?"

Dash shot up in the air. "Sure as sugar!" she exclaimed.

"What an honor," Berry added. "We'd love to."

Princess Lolli smiled. "I was hoping you'd agree to that," she said. "Thank you."

Berry wondered if Princess Lolli was hoping that Princess Mini would be a Fruit Fairy like her. Berry was *definitely* hoping the new royal would be just like her, but she didn't want to say anything to her friends. If Mini were a

Fruit Fairy, Berry imagined how they would spend time together in Fruit Chew Meadow or Lollipop Landing.

"Berry!" Cocoa said, tapping her arm. "Please pass the tea." She nudged her friend. "What were you thinking about? I was trying to get your attention."

"Sorry," Berry said. She passed Cocoa the teapot, smiling to herself about her secret thoughts.

CHAPTER 3

A Royal Sleepover

The Candy Fairies arrived at Candy Castle early the next morning. Nothing was better than a royal sleepover! The five friends couldn't keep their wings still. They were buzzing with the excitement of being fairy-sitters for the next two days.

Two castles guards showed them to their

guest room. The friends were sharing a room on the same floor as Princess Mini's nursery. The room was very big and very pink. Berry loved all the prints of candy on the wall and the sweet smell of cotton candy. "This is *sugar-tastic*!" she exclaimed.

"Royal living is sweet," Raina said.

Berry dragged the last of her large, over-stuffed bags into the room. "That's all of it," she said, sinking down into a chair.

"We aren't staying for a month," Melli said. She looked down at the one bag she had packed for the sleepover.

Berry shrugged. "You know I have to be pre-pared," she said. "A fairy needs outfit choices."

"And sweet snacks," Dash said, pulling open her basket of minty treats.

Raina unzipped her bag and took out a huge stack of books. "I brought a couple books for Princess Mini," she said.

"A couple?" Cocoa said, laughing. "You'll have to read to her every hour for the whole time we're here! You brought an entire library."

"I'd be happy to read her these books," Raina said. "I already know she loves stories."

Dash rolled her eyes. "You know there *is* a library in the castle," she said.

Raina patted her books. "I know," she said. "But these are some of my favorites. I wanted to be sure to read her these. Especially at bedtime."

Melli took out her licorice stick from her bag. "And I brought my music," she said. "I know Mini loves when I play songs. I've been practicing a lullaby."

"I have art supplies," Cocoa said. She pointed to a bag. "Mini may be little but I know she loves art."

Berry smiled. "We are the best fairysitters ever!"

"I hope Mini will be happy with us watching her while her parents are away," Melli said. She twirled a piece of hair around her finger. "I know she is used to seeing us, but I'm still worried she might cry."

"Babies cry," Princess Lolli said. She flew into the room and hugged them all. "I know Mini is going to love having you here to entertain her. Just look at all the stuff you have to keep her busy!"

"We're excited," Raina told her.

"Wait till Mini sees you all here," Princess Lolli said. "She is going to be so happy. Prince Scoop is getting her up from her nap. They will be here any minute."

Berry kept her eyes on the door. She couldn't wait for her fairysitting responsibilities to begin.

"The Castle Fairies are here if you need them," Princess Lolli told them. "They are busy with preparations for Mini's ball, so you are on Mini watch. You've done this before, so I know you know Mini's routine and what she likes and doesn't like. Your responsibility is to make sure she is safe and happy."

"Sure as sugar, we'll watch her and make sure she has the sweetest time," Dash said.

"I know," Princess Lolli said. "That is why we picked you for the job."

Prince Scoop flew in with Princess Mini. She was squirming around in his arms. "Look who is up and ready to play," he said.

The five friends flew over to see the little royal cutie.

The prince kissed his daughter on the forehead and placed her on a blanket. "We have to be on our way, but we'll see you in two days!"

Princess Lolli gave Mini a tight hug and whispered in her ear. Berry could tell it was hard for her to leave her baby.

"Be a sweet," Princess Lolli said. "And have fun being fairysitters," she called to the Candy Fairies. "We will be in touch."

"Have fun," Prince Scoop said as he took Princess Lolli's hand.

When the royal couple left, Berry looked to her friends. Raina took out one of her books and Mini clapped her hands. She recognized the pictures and story. Raina gave Mini a gummy flower with a chocolate petal to chew on. Princess Mini clapped again and eagerly ate her snack. "More, more," she said, pulling at the book.

Raina grinned. "See, I told you she loved books."

"And sweet treats," Dash added, smiling.

As Raina read the story about a baby gummy bear, Princess Mini licked the chocolate petals. At the end of the story, she sneezed. Three times. The last one was the loudest!

"ACHOOOOO!"

"Are you all right?" Raina asked the baby princess. She closed the book and looked at Mini.

"More, more," Mini said. She pointed to the book and went back to nibbling on her gummy flower.

"I guess she's fine," Dash whispered. "Keep reading."

"Achooooo! Achooooo! ACHOOOO!"

Princess Mini's nose was red and her sneezing got louder and louder with each sneeze.

"Oh no," Melli moaned. "What do we do if Princess Mini is sick?"

Berry looked over at Mini. "I hope she isn't getting sick!" She looked into the baby's blue eyes. "Are you feeling okay?"

Princess Mini looked up at Berry and smiled. "Bee-Bee," she said. "Berry!"

"Did she just say 'Berry'?" Dash said.

Berry thought her heart would burst. "She did! And she is smiling. She doesn't seem sick. In fact, she seems perfect!" She gave the baby a tight squeeze and Princess Mini giggled.

"Nothing better than a baby princess hug," Berry said, grinning.

Just then a sugar fly swooped in through the castle window and landed on Raina's shoulder. Raina read the message and then gasped. "There is a gummy flower meltdown in Gummy Forest. I need to go and help out."

"Achooooo! Achooooo! ACHOOOO!"

Princess Mini sneezed again. She was smiling and didn't look upset, but those sneezes made her fairysitters nervous.

"She's fine," Berry said. "Raina, go see what the trouble is and we'll put Mini to bed. No need to worry. A couple sneezes doesn't mean she's sick."

As Raina flew off to see what the sugar fly message was all about, Berry hoped that what she'd said was true and that Princess Mini was not getting sick. No one wanted a sick baby fairy princess right before her first ball!

Red Sour Cherry

After sneezing at least ten times, Princess Mini went to sleep. Raina returned after Princess Mini had fallen asleep and reported that everything was all right in Gummy Forest. Their first day as fairysitters had a little excitement, but the evening had gone well.

The next day, the sunrise in the sky was

a delicious lemon-yellow and orange burst. Berry got up early and went to Fruit Chew Meadow to pick some juicy treats before breakfast.

When Berry arrived at the meadow, she saw that Raina was already there. She flew over to her. "Is everything all right?" she asked. "What are *you* doing here so early?"

"I couldn't sleep," Raina told her. "I felt terrible about Mini's sneezes yesterday. I want to make sure that she has the best time today—and the best candy to eat."

"I know what you mean," Berry said. "I thought I was the first one up this morning. I never get up so early!"

"Did you finish sewing Mini's cape last night?" Raina asked.

Last night Berry had put the finishing touches on a new outfit she made for Princess Mini. She had been saving the sweet grape sugar cloth for something special and made the princess a royal cape. Berry was sure that Mini would love the soft material and the rainbow cotton candy collar. The cape would be so pretty against Mini's strawberry blonde hair.

"I did," Berry told her. "I can't wait for her to try it on." She flew over to a cherry blossom and smelled the sweet scent. "Yum! We made these fruit chews together so they will be double sweet for Princess Mini."

The two friends picked all the ripe candies off the vine until both of their baskets were full.

"What should we do this afternoon with Mini?" Raina asked.

Berry snatched one more orange chew and put it in her basket. "We should go for a fly in the Royal Gardens," she said. "The fresh air will be good for her."

Raina agreed. "That sounds like a *sugar-tastic* plan!"

"Look at this," Berry said, pointing to a puddle of melted gummy flowers. "There hasn't been any rain or extreme weather. I wonder why this vine is all melted."

"Sometimes there's a random melt," Raina said, shrugging her shoulders. "At least it doesn't look as bad as the Gummy Forest did yesterday."

A small sugar fly landed on Berry's shoulder. "This must be Cocoa wondering when we are coming back," she said.

"Or Dash hoping we bring back some candy for her!" Raina said, laughing.

Berry laughed. "Now that wouldn't surprise me," she said. But she stopped laughing when she read the note. "Oh no!" she exclaimed.

"What's wrong?" Raina asked.

"Melli says we must return to the castle right away," Berry read. "The sneezing is back and Princess Mini had a chocolate-caramel lollipop and now has red sour-cherry cheeks!"

The two Candy Fairies flew back quickly and arrived to find Dash, Cocoa, and Melli circling Princess Mini's crib.

Melli turned to them and put her finger to her lips. "Shhh," she said. "Princess Mini is finally asleep."

Raina flew over to the crib.

The baby looked cozy and peaceful. "Her cheeks aren't red," she whispered. "You called us back to see her sleeping?"

"Things were a little different a while ago," Dash said. She quietly sat down on a lemon-colored pouf chair.

Berry shook her head. "She seems fine now," she said. "I don't think we should worry anyone. Maybe it's normal for the baby to have red checks."

"I don't know," Dash said slowly. "You didn't see those red cheeks. They were sour-cherry red. It was not pretty."

Raina shook her head. "Well, her cheeks look fine now and she's resting," she said to Melli.

"Let's not argue," Melli said. "We don't want

to upset Mini." She motioned to the room off the nursery. "Let's sit in our room so we don't wake her."

"Melli has a point," Cocoa said, flying into their room. "I'm exhausted from entertaining her all morning. We read books, sang songs, and played some games. Baby fairy princesses are a lot of work. I think Melli, Dash, and I used up all our tricks."

Berry put down her basket of fresh fruit chews. "How about we go for a fly in the Royal Gardens?" she said. She flew over and took out the purple cape. "And Princess Mini can wear this!"

"Oh, Berry!" Melli exclaimed. "That is beautiful!"

"She's going to love that," Cocoa said.

"I want one of those," Dash told Berry. She reached out to feel the soft fabric. "Oh, I love how it feels!"

Berry smiled. "Thank you," she said. "I hope Mini likes it."

"*Achoooo! Achooo! ACHOOOOO!*"

"And she's up!" Cocoa said.

The friends flew over to the crib and saw Princess Mini sitting up with the reddest cheeks Berry had ever seen. "Oh, sweet strawberries," she said. "Is that what you saw before?"

"Yup," Melli said. "Now you see why we sent the sugar fly to you."

"We have to tell the Castle Fairies and call the doctor," Raina said. "Poor Princess Mini."

"I'll go find one of the Castle Fairies," Cocoa

said as she flew quickly down the hall.

"Bee-Bee," Princess Mini chanted. "Berry!"

Melli tapped Berry. "She's asking for you," she said.

"Maybe she wants that purple cape," Dash said. "Look how she's reaching for it."

Princess Mini's eyes were focused on the cape in Berry's hands. Berry rushed over and draped the cape around the baby's shoulders.

The color was perfect for the little princess. She cooed when she felt the soft fabric. Berry touched her red cheek.

Cocoa flew back into the room. "I asked Snaps, one of the Castle Fairies, to call Dr. Spice," she said. "Snaps said the doctor will be here shortly."

"Let's hope Dr. Spice knows what is going on with Mini," Berry said. "Poor Princess Mini!"

"Mini doesn't look sick," Dash said. "She looks super stylish in that cape."

"But those cheeks," Berry said. "There's something not right. She picked up the baby and gave her a hug. "The doctor is coming soon," she said. "Just hold on."

5

Dr. Spice & Everything Nice

Princess Mini had stopped sneezing, but her cheeks were still very, very red. She fell asleep in her crib wearing Berry's purple cape. The five fairysitters were quietly flying circles in the room while they waited for the royal doctor to arrive.

"Where is Dr. Spice?" Melli asked. She looked out the large castle window. "She should be here already."

There was a knock on the door. "I hope that's Dr. Spice," Dash said. She was the first one to the door.

"Oh, I didn't know you would be here, Princess Dash," Dr. Spice said when she saw Dash open the door. She bowed and looked a little flustered. "It is an honor to meet you, Princess Dash."

Dash turned peppermint red. Many fairies in Sugar Valley knew the story of how Dash had become a princess. The story of the long lost Peppermint princess was big news in Sugar Valley. Dash didn't like people recognizing her and becoming flustered when they spoke to her. "I'm not the princess you need to be concerned about," she said.

"Dash," Raina scolded her. "Don't be rude."

"I'm sorry," Dash said to Dr. Spice. She took the doctor's hand. "Please stop bowing to me. We are very worried about Princess Mini. Her cheeks have been turning red after she sneezes. We aren't sure what is happening."

"Let me examine her and I will let you know," Dr. Spice told the fairies. "Please wait outside the room. I will come get you when I am done."

Berry wanted to stay with Mini, but she followed her friends out the door to the hallway.

"I hope Mini is all right," Cocoa said.

"She's in good hands," Raina told her.

"I still can't get used to people calling me *princess*," Dash said. She got up and flew back and forth in the hallway. "And all that bowing business makes me very uncomfortable."

"But it *is* your name and your title!" Raina told her. "Fairies are taught to bow to royalty. It's a sign of respect."

Dash shook her head. "It still feels funny," she said. "Especially here at Candy Castle where there is another super royal family."

"Any royal is a super royal," Berry said. She glared at her minty royal friend. "Dash, please sit still. Your fluttering wings are making me nervous!"

Dash landed and sat down with her back against the wall. "I'm sorry," she said. "My wings just start to move when I feel nervous."

Melli sat down next to Dash. "I'm sorry," she said. "We're all worried about Princess Mini." She looked at Dash's face. "It must be strange for you to have people treat you differently now that you are a princess."

"I just wish fairies knew that I am still the same old Candy Fairy as before," Dash said. "Sure, I have a kingdom now and everything, but I'm still *me*."

"With a title and a crown," Berry added. Then she smiled. "You are still my good old minty Dash. Sure as sugar, that will never change."

"Thanks," Dash said. "I think," she added with a giggle. "Thanks for being such supersweet friends. Coming back to Candy Kingdom and being with all of you is really important to me."

"We wouldn't have it any other way," Melli told her.

"We will always be here for you, Dash," Raina said. "Princess Dash, that is." She flew over and gave Dash a tight squeeze.

Cocoa flew to the princess's door. "I wonder what Dr. Spice is saying to Mini. Do you think she woke her up?"

Raina stood. "Princess Mini is a healthy baby," she said. "She's going to be fine."

Melli twirled her hair around her finger. "She *was* a healthy baby when her parents last saw her," she whispered. "Oh, we should have sent a sugar fly to Princess Lolli."

"Let's wait until we know what to tell her," Cocoa said. "If this is serious, the doctor will let us know."

"I can't keep still!" Dash exclaimed. "I have go check."

"Me too!" Berry said, leaping up.

"If you're going in, we're all going in," Melli said.

Just then, the door opened and Dr. Spice flew out of the room. "Princess Mini went back to sleep," she said quietly. "She is having an allergic reaction to something." She looked at the five fairysitters. "I took a test and I will fly back tomorrow with the results." The doctor sighed. "She will be fine." She looked around at the five Candy Fairies. "No need for such worried faces!"

"Her parents are away," Raina said. "We need to send a sugar fly message."

"I have already done that," Dr. Spice told them. "Don't worry. Princess Mini is not in any danger. She just needs some rest. And some loving fairysitters."

"We can be loving fairysitters!" Berry said.

"I am sure of that," Dr. Spice said. "Please keep a list of things she eats. This reaction has something to do with what she is eating. Don't worry, this is nothing that serious, but we need to find out what is making her sneeze. I will be back. Remember, you can always reach me by sugar fly." She looked over at Dash and bowed her head. "Good day, Princess Dash."

Dash nodded. Berry thought her friend seemed a bit more comfortable, and she was glad.

"I know just the thing to help Princess Mini," Cocoa said. She snapped her fingers and her eyes sparkled. "I'm not sure why I didn't think of this before!"

"What?" Melli asked.

"An old Chocolate Fairy trick," Cocoa said. "I know it will work."

Berry raised her dark eyebrows. She wasn't sure that Cocoa's chocolate trick would work.

"It's worth a try," Cocoa said, looking at Berry. "I'll be back before Sun Dip!"

Berry was unsure about Cocoa's chocolate thinking. "We'll see," she said. She took out a notepad and began writing down what she remembered the princess eating. She wanted to figure out what was making her sneeze!

6

Chocolate Trick

By the time Cocoa returned, Berry had written out all the foods and treats Princess Mini had eaten since Princess Lolli and Prince Scoop left. She kept staring at the list, hoping to see what might be causing the sneezes.

"Nothing seems out of the ordinary," Berry said to Raina. "She's had all these foods before."

"Sometimes allergies just happen," Raina said.

"I have found the cure to Princess Mini's sneezes!" Cocoa said, flying into the nursery with a bottle.

"What?" Dash asked.

"I went to the Chocolate Woods," Cocoa said. She shook the bottle in her hand. "I made some special chocolate milk. It's the best cure of all."

Berry flew over to Cocoa. "But Dr. Spice didn't mention giving her anything like this," she told Cocoa.

"I'm sure it can't hurt," Cocoa said.

"Write it down on the list," Melli said.

Cocoa shook the bottle and flew over to Mini's crib. "This milk always made me feel better when I was little," she said. "Mini's had this treat before, but never fresh from the woods like this!"

Berry looked over at Raina. She was very quiet. "What do you think?" Berry asked her.

Raina shrugged. "I guess it wouldn't hurt to try," she said. "Dr. Spice didn't say *not* to give Mini anything. She just said to write it down." She pulled out a straw from a basket by her bed. "Here, put this caramel straw in the bottle for Mini. This will make it easier for her to drink."

Berry stood back as her friends gathered around Princess Mini's crib. She didn't like the idea that Cocoa had gotten something for Mini first. Berry had thought that she would get Mini a fruity drink. She, too, had had

favorite drinks from when she was a young fairy and not feeling well.

"Mini likes it!" Cocoa cheered. She beamed as Princess Mini cooed and drank up her chocolate milk.

"You don't have to be so proud of yourself," Berry mumbled.

Cocoa turned to glare at her. "Why are you so sour?" she asked.

"I'm not sour," Berry snapped.

"Stop bickering, you two," Melli said, holding up her hands. "Fairysitters are supposed to watch out for one another."

"And their fairy," Raina said, peering into the crib. "Princess Mini seems all right. She drank the chocolate milk."

"See, I told you," Cocoa said proudly.

Berry narrowed her eyes. She didn't mean to be so sassy. She never thought chocolate milk would be the answer!

"Mini does seem happy," Melli reported.

Berry flew over to Princess Mini and handed her a small stuffed fairy doll. The doll was wearing a beautiful pink-and-white dress, and had the same color hair as Mini.

"Holy peppermint!" Dash squealed. "That doll is *sugar-tastic*! You made it?"

"I did," Berry said. "I had one just like that when I was small. I used to make dresses for a doll just like this one." She held up a few dresses in a rainbow of colors with tiny sugar crystals.

"Of all the dolls you've given the princess, this one wins the prize," Dash said.

Princess Mini reached out and kissed the doll on the head. The little princess looked up at Berry. "Thank you, Berry!" she said.

"She said my name again!" Berry cheered. She scooped up the princess in her arms. She snuggled her close and then held her up.

"Achoooo! Achooo! ACHOOOOO!"

Princess Mini was at it again!

"Oh no!" Berry said. "Her cheeks are so red and now there are tiny bumps! I don't think the chocolate milk helped."

"Those are hives!" Raina said. "That comes from an allergy. Poor Mini."

A sugar fly came into the nursery and landed on Melli's shoulder. "I am afraid to read this note," she said. "The last sugar fly was bad news about Gummy Forest." She handed the letter to Raina.

"Looks like a Caramel Hills meltdown is happening," Raina said as she read the note. "Melli, this is from Cara and she needs your help."

Cara was Melli's younger sister. She would not have sent for Melli if there wasn't a real emergency in Caramel Hills.

"What is going on?" Cocoa asked. "It's one disaster after another since we came here to watch Mini."

"Maybe there's a curse!" Melli gasped.

Raina shook her head. "No, but I am beginning to think that Mini's sneezes are more powerful than we thought."

Berry nodded her head. "Each time Mini has sneezed, some place in the kingdom has had a meltdown," she said. "First Gummy Forest, then Fruit Chew Meadow, and now Caramel Hills.

"Melli, you should go," Raina said, putting a hand on her friend's shoulder. "We'll watch Mini and send for Dr. Spice."

Melli kissed Mini on her forehead and flew out behind the tiny sugar fly. "Send me a message when you know something. I'm going to Caramel Hills. Cara and the other Caramel Fairies are sure to be in a real sticky mess."

A castle guard knocked on the door. He stuck his head in the room. "Princess Lolli and Prince Scoop are coming home tomorrow," he said. "The royal couple wanted me to tell you to keep Mini comfortable until they return." He closed the door and the Candy Fairies looked at Princess Mini.

"I guess bad news travels as fast as good news," Dash said.

"Maybe even faster," Cocoa said, looking down. "I feel terrible that the chocolate milk not only didn't work, but might have made things worse."

"Mini doesn't look uncomfortable or sad," Raina said.

"Thanks, Raina," Cocoa replied, "but I still feel responsible."

Berry stood up. "We are all responsible for Mini," she said. "Our job as fairysitters is to make sure she stays safe."

"What are we going to do about her sneezing and red bumps?" Dash asked.

"Dash, you and I will get Dr. Spice," Raina said, thinking of a plan on the spot. "I can't just wait around for her to return."

Dash jumped up. "We can fly faster than any sugar fly," she said.

"We can grab a few more books from the castle library," Raina added. "We have to find out what is making the princess sneeze so much."

"We'll get to the bottom of this, I promise," Berry said, looking down at Mini.

Princess Mini looked up and waved her

fairy doll. She sneezed three more times and Berry looked over at Dash, Raina, and Cocoa.

"You better fly fast," Berry said to Raina and Dash. "I think we need to prepare for another meltdown!"

"We'll be back!" Raina called, as she and Dash went to find Dr. Spice.

7

Fruit-Chew Hopes

Berry and Cocoa tried to keep Mini busy while they waited for Raina and Dash to return to the castle with Dr. Spice. Cocoa showed the princess how to use colorful icings to finger paint and read her a story about a baby gnome. Berry changed the dress on the fairy doll a few times and then set up a grand royal tea party.

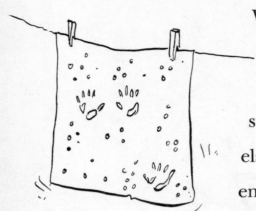

When Dr. Spice was still not there, the two fairysitters were stuck thinking of what else they could do to entertain Mini.

"I wish we could take Mini out to the Royal Gardens," Cocoa said.

Berry shook her head. "What if she started sneezing again? And her cheeks turned red? The *Daily Scoop* would be all over that news story!"

"You're right," Cocoa said. She took out colorful blocks from her bag. Mini started to stack the blocks and Cocoa sighed. "I wonder what is taking them so long to get Dr. Spice."

"I'm not sure," she said. "It feels like a long

time." She looked over at Mini. "Fairysitting is hard work!"

"Bee-Bee!" Mini said. She changed her fairy doll's dress and took another piece of material to make a head wrap. She held up her doll for Berry to see and then placed her in a throne made from Cocoa's blocks.

"I think that Mini loves fashion as much as you do," Cocoa said. "She has that fashion sense already."

Berry smiled. She knew the princess was enjoying the doll and the dresses. Every time Berry saw Mini, she would bring her a doll. Mini's eyes lit up when Berry handed her a doll with new handmade outfits, which was exactly how Berry had reacted when she had been a little fairy too. Once again, Berry thought how *sugar-tastic* it would be if the newest royal were a Fruit Fairy. When Berry was a year old, she had touched the sugar in the sugar bowl and fruit chews had appeared. Maybe Mini would create fruit chews too.

"Achoo! Achooooo! ACHOOOOOOO!"

"Oh, poor you!" Berry said. She didn't like the princess sneezing and getting red bumps on her sweet cheeks. She checked the food list. The last thing Mini had eaten was chocolate cereal.

Snaps came into the nursery. "Is everything all right?" she asked. She flew over to Mini.

"Raina and Dash have gone to get Dr. Spice," Cocoa told her.

"I am sure once Dr. Spice gets here, she'll know what to do," Snaps said. "I'll be here if you need me. Mini is happy playing with you. Thank you for watching over her."

When Snaps left, Cocoa flew closer to Berry. "I hope I didn't make Mini worse by giving her chocolate milk," she said.

"She doesn't seem worse," Berry said. "We have to stay positive."

Cocoa squinted out the window. "Wait! I see Dash!" she exclaimed, flying closer to the window. She pointed up to the sky.

"Dash is definitely a faster flyer than any sugar fly!" Berry said. She picked up Princess Mini and flew to the window next to Cocoa. "Raina and Dr. Spice are behind her," Berry added. She turned to Mini. "Dr. Spice is coming!"

"Bee-Bee, Berrrrry!" Princess Mini said.

Berry thought her heart would melt. "That's right," she said. "I am Berry. And we're all here to find out what is making you sneeze. Your sneezes are making a big old mess."

Dash flew in first with a basket in her hand. "I brought these mint ice cream sandwiches," she said. "Dr. Spice thought it would be a good idea to see if Mini liked them. You know they always helped me feel minty good." She opened the basket and held one up for Princess Mini. "Would you like one?"

Princess Mini clapped her hands and reached for the cold treat.

"That was a good answer!" Dash exclaimed. She handed the small princess the ice cream sandwich.

The princess's nose wrinkled up when her

tongue touched the cold ice cream. Then a smile spread across her face. The sweet mint made her coo happily.

"I think she likes the treat," Cocoa said.

Raina and Dr. Spice arrived as Mini was finishing her ice cream sandwich. Dr. Spice took Mini in her arms. "The good news is Princess Mini is not in any danger," Dr. Spice said. "I spoke to her parents last night and this morning. They are eager to see her today and to find out what is making her sneeze."

"Achoo! Achoooooo! ACHOOOOOOOO!"

"Bitter mint," Dash said, her wings dropping low to the ground. "I guess those ice cream sandwiches weren't so minty good for Princess Mini."

"You're right that she doesn't seem bothered

by the sneezing or the red bumps on her cheeks," Dr. Spice said. "I am glad about that." She looked over at Berry. "Has the princess had a fruit nectar drink?"

"Actually, she hasn't had any fruit candy or a fruit drink since we've been here," Berry said, checking her list. "Do you think she should have some? I was planning on getting some fruit nectar earlier today, but then the chocolate milk and the mint ice cream made things worse."

"Hmm," Dr. Spice said. "I think that a sip of fruit nectar is worth a try."

Cocoa turned to the window. "Sure as sugar, here comes a message. Just as we suspected. Each time there are sneezes, there is a mess somewhere!"

"Yes," Dr. Spice said. "I'm not surprised. These types of allergies usually have some magical mess that goes along with sneezes and red cheeks."

"The sugar fly has a message for you, Dash," Cocoa said. "It's addressed to Princess Dash."

Dash rolled her eyes. "It's going to be bad news," she said. She quickly read the note. "A Peppermint Grove minty problem," Dash said. "I have to help out."

Berry turned to Raina. "Maybe Princess Mini is a Fruit Fairy," she said. "There has been a problem in every area of Sugar Valley except in the fruity places. There was a little fruit chew melt in Fruit Chew Meadow, but nothing like what has been happening in Gummy Forest, Caramel Hills, and Peppermint Grove."

"That might be true," Dr. Spice said. "Go get some fruit nectar, Berry. The fruit might help Princess Mini."

Berry flew quickly toward Fruit Chew Meadow where she knew she could get some fresh fruit nectar for the princess. Berry wanted to be the one to find the cure for the sneezing princess, and a sweet fruit drink might just be part of that cure. Maybe those royal fruit chews were possible.

8

Fruity Patience

When Berry got to Fruit Chew Meadow, she had to work quickly. There was a combination of fruits she wanted to mix for Princess Mini. She knew that the juices of strawberry and cherry would make a sweet red drink for her. Adding some extra fruit chews would make the drink perfect.

Berry held up the juice in a bottle. She had to make sure the color was just right. She picked a fresh fruit chew off the vine and thought about what else she needed. "The straw!" she exclaimed. She flew off to Licorice Lake to get a thick piece of licorice for the princess's straw.

"Hi, Fruli!" Berry called when she saw her Fruit Fairy friend on the red sands of Licorice Lake. Fruli was a very fancy Fruit Fairy from Meringue Island. Berry always loved seeing her and hearing about the latest fashions from Meringue Island. She used to be very jealous of her, but now the two were good friends.

Fruli flew over to Berry and gave her a hug. "I've been thinking about you," she said. "How is Princess Mini? Are you having the best time being a fairysitter? I know you love spending time with her."

Berry sighed. "I am, except Princess Mini keeps sneezing," she told her. "And each time she sneezes, there is some kind of candy melt mess in Sugar Valley."

"That is strange," Fruli said. "What does Dr. Spice think?"

"She thinks it might be an allergic reaction," Berry said. "I thought I'd bring Mini back some red fruit nectar to see if that helps."

Fruli looked at the bottle in Berry's hands. "Oh, that looks *sugar-tastic*," she said. "I'm sure that will help her."

"I am looking for the perfect licorice stalk for the straw," Berry said. "Want to help me look?"

"Sure," Fruli replied. "I finished gathering some thin licorice ropes to make a swing for Princess Mini. I wanted to give her something special for her birthday."

Berry saw the long red licorice ropes in Fruli's basket. "Mini is going to love a swing!" she exclaimed. She saw the perfect stalk for the straw. "How about this one?"

"She'll love it," Fruli told her. "I hope the princess feels better. Do you think she will be fine for her party tomorrow?"

"Yes," Berry said. "She will be."

And then Berry had a terrible thought. *What if Princess Mini had gotten worse while she was out? What would happen if she were too sick to go to her ball?*

"I have to get back," Berry told Fruli. "I'll

see you later." She quickly took off and headed to the castle.

On the way, Berry thought about what would happen if Princess Mini were sick for the party. There would be no sugar bowl touch! The thought was so sour that Berry couldn't think about it. Maybe the fruit nectar in her bag would help and all this sneezing would end. She hoped once Princess Mini discovered her candy talent, this messy allergy would go away.

When Berry returned to the nursery, Princess Mini was napping. The room was quiet, and Raina, Cocoa, and Dash were all reading large books from the castle library. Dr. Spice was studying a scroll in the corner of the room and looked up to wave to Berry.

"Hello, Berry," Dr. Spice said. "All is well. The sneezing has stopped."

Berry was happy to hear that news. At least things hadn't gotten worse. "I have the fruit nectar," Berry told her. She held up the bright red juice with the fresh licorice straw.

"That looks like the color of Princess Mini's cheeks!" Dash cried.

Berry gave Dash a side glance. "The strawberry and cherry mix is very healing and delicious," she said.

"Yes, this is perfect, Berry," Dr. Spice said. She woke Mini, who took a few sips of the nectar. "Princess Lolli and Prince Scoop will return in a little while. Unfortunately we need to wait and see if Mini still has a reaction to certain foods. I don't have a real answer as to why she is sneezing and getting those red cheeks."

Berry peered over Dr. Spice's shoulder. "Is Princess Mini a Fruit Fairy?" she blurted out.

Raina, Dash, and Cocoa gasped as they looked toward Dr. Spice. Even for the bold Berry, that comment was not what they expected.

Berry's face turned as red as the juice in the bottle. "You see," she started to explain, "so far all the things Princess Mini ate had some chocolate in them. There was the chocolate-covered gummy, a chocolate-caramel lollipop, the chocolate milk, and the chocolate cookies in the ice cream sandwich." She looked at her friends and then back at Dr. Spice. "The fruit nectar was the only non-chocolate thing!"

"She's right about that," Dash said.

"Could she be allergic to chocolate?" Melli asked.

Dash gasped. "How awful," she said.

"Maybe not," Berry added. "Dr. Spice?"

Dr. Spice rolled up the scroll she had been reading. "I need to wait for her parents to discuss her sugar talent," she said, "and what is happening."

"But . . . ," Berry began, but Raina took her hand and gave it a tight squeeze.

"We need to wait, Berry," she told her. "Fruity patience!"

"I know what is happening here," Berry whispered to Raina. "Princess Mini is a Fruit Fairy. I am sure of it."

Raina looked at her and smiled. "No one

knows yet. We have to wait," she said. "It doesn't matter what Princess Mini's talent is as long as she's okay."

Berry knew what Raina was saying. Of course she just wanted the princess to be healthy. But she wanted to know if the sweet baby princess was a Fruit Fairy like her. She couldn't wait for Princess Lolli and Prince Scoop to return to Candy Castle.

9

A Sweet Talent

As soon as Princess Lolli and Prince Scoop returned from Cake Kingdom, Dr. Spice asked to speak to the royal parents alone. Berry tried to keep herself busy by finishing up the jeweled collar on Melli's dress for the ball. Now all five dresses were complete. She looked up at the closed door across the hall.

She and her friends had been sitting in their room. "I can't wait out here any longer," Berry said. "What is Dr. Spice saying to them?"

Melli flew down the hall. She was just returning from Caramel Hills. "Is there any news?" she called to her friends.

"Not yet," Dash told her. "How are things in Caramel Hills?"

"A bit sticky," Melli said. "But everything is all cleaned up now. It wasn't so bad with everyone helping to clean up the melted mess." She turned to Dash. "And in Peppermint Grove?"

"Minty fresh," Dash said. "No one even called me princess. It was nice to work in the grove again with the other Mint Candy Fairies." She looked toward the closed nursery door. "Do you think the ball will still happen? The party is supposed to be tomorrow."

"I've been thinking the same thing," Berry said. With all the sneezing and the messes around Sugar Valley, she wasn't sure the ball would happen.

"That would be very sour," Melli said. "Everyone has been looking forward to the ball."

"And to learning Princess Mini's candy talent," Cocoa said.

Berry tapped her foot. She was getting nervous listening to her friends. She hoped that the ball wouldn't be canceled. And more than anything she hoped that Princess Mini would be declared a Fruit Fairy. "I hope Dr. Spice has good news," she said.

"Wait, I think I hear something," Raina said.

She flew closer to the nursery door. "They're coming!"

The door opened. Princess Lolli stood in the doorway holding Mini in her arms. The baby was smiling and waving a cupcake rattle.

"Come in," Princess Lolli told the Candy Fairies. "There is some good news to share."

After waiting so long, it was nice to see both Princess Mini and Princess Lolli smiling. The five friends flew into the nursery and saw Dr. Spice and Prince Scoop shaking hands.

"Thank you so much," Prince Scoop said to Dr. Spice. He had a smile on his face so wide that Berry knew there was extra-happy news to share.

"Dr. Spice's tests show that Princess Mini has choco-fever," Princess Lolli said. "This is

very common for royal Candy Fairy babies. She had allergic reactions to chocolate, but it isn't permanent."

"Dr. Spice has given Mini some medicine so those powerful sneezes will stop," Prince Scoop added.

"So is she a Candy Fairy or an Ice Cream Fairy?" Raina said, leaning forward.

"A Chocolate Candy Fairy?" Cocoa asked, grinning proudly.

Berry watched Dr. Spice as she nodded. "Yes and yes," she said. "Princess Mini is a Chocolate Candy Fairy, but she will also have the power to make ice cream. This is a power that she will grow into. Time will tell what kind of ice cream she will create." She smiled. "And we still need to wait for the sugar bowl touch to know what candy she will create."

"*So mint!*" Dash cheered.

"*Sugar-tastic!*" Raina cried.

"Supersweet," Cocoa said.

Melli picked up her licorice stick and played a happy melody. Everyone in the room was flying and celebrating except for Berry.

"Berry, are you all right?" Princess Lolli asked. She pulled Berry aside.

"Yes," Berry said, forcing a smile. "I'm so happy that Princess Mini is all right." She took a deep breath. "It's just. . . . Well, um . . . ," she tried to get the words out. "I thought she was going to be a Fruit Fairy," she said quickly.

Princess Lolli nodded. "I know," she said. "But Princess Mini can learn so much from you. She doesn't have to be just like you *or* me."

Berry saw that Princess Lolli understood. After all, Princess Lolli was a Fruit Fairy too. "Are you sad that Mini isn't a Fruit Fairy?" Berry asked.

"I'm happy that she's healthy," the princess told her. "And I am a bit surprised to learn that her talent will be chocolate, but I am happy for her. Being a Chocolate Fairy is really fun and I know she will make an excellent one."

"You're right," Berry said. She looked at Princess Mini. The baby wrinkled her nose and pointed at Berry. "Beeerrrry!" she said, stretching out her arms.

"I think she wants to play," Princess Lolli said. She flew over to Mini and then placed her down on a blanket. Mini picked up her

fairy doll and gave it a big hug. "She loves this doll you made her, Berry."

Berry laughed. She watched how Mini played with the doll. She sat down on the blanket and played with her.

"Princess Lolli, is the ball still happening?" Melli asked. "We were wondering."

"Sure as sugar," Princess Lolli said, reaching down and scooping up the baby. "This little one has a big day ahead of her tomorrow."

Berry glanced over at her friends. With all the sneezing and candy messes to clean up, they had forgotten their promise of getting the sugar for the sugar bowl!

CHAPTER 10

Sugar Bowl Surprise

Berry signaled to Raina and Cocoa to get Dash and Melli's attention. In a flash, the five fairies were out the window of Princess Mini's nursery.

"Princess Mini should rest, so we'll be going," Berry called over her shoulder. "We'll be back soon!"

"What is the big emergency?" Dash asked when they were outside.

"The sugar for the sugar bowl!" Berry exclaimed. "We forgot to get the sugar!"

"Holy mint!" Dash exclaimed. "How could we have forgotten such an important task?"

Cocoa shrugged. "We have been a little busy," she said.

"We'd be in sticky syrup if we showed up to the ball *without* the sugar for the sugar bowl!" Raina said.

Berry waved her friends on to follow her. "We have to get to the sugar mines now," she said. "Only the cleanest sugar should be used."

"You're right," Raina said. "Let's go."

The five friends flew to the sugar mines at

the end of Caramel Hills. They each took a sack of the finest sugar.

"What kind of chocolate do you think she'll make?" Dash asked.

"I made chocolate squares," Cocoa boasted. "But in time, Mini will learn all different kinds of chocolate candies."

Berry couldn't help feeling a tiny bit sad. She wished that she could be imagining the type of fruit candy that the princess would make at her party. But then she watched her friends giggling and talking together: none of them had the same talent, and yet they were all such good friends. She felt her wings relax and she flew over to join in on the fun.

They delivered the sugar to one of the castle guards. Now that it was midday, Berry knew Princess Mini would be ready to take a stroll in the gardens.

"Let's go see if we can take Princess Mini out before she needs to get ready for the party," Berry said.

"And before we have to get ready!" Melli exclaimed. "I'm going to need time to get dressed."

"Me too," Berry said, giggling.

Princess Lolli was happy to see the Candy Fairies in the nursery. "I would love you to take Princess Mini outside for a little while," she said. "Now that Mini is feeling better, she should get some fresh air." She wrapped Mini in her new purple cape.

Berry was full of pride. She felt good that Princess Lolli had chosen Berry's cape for

Princess Mini to wear at the ball. She went to help her with the royal carriage.

"You know," Princess Lolli said softly to Berry, "she may not be a Fruit Fairy, but that doesn't mean you can't teach her things."

Berry smiled. "Thank you for saying that," she said. "I guess my hopes for another Fruit Fairy royal were a bit too high."

Princess Lolli put Mini in her stroller. "You have a special place in her heart already," she said. "Thank you for taking such great care of her." She turned to the others. "Have her back before her midday nap," she told the fairysitters.

"Sure as sugar," Berry sang out.

They flew out the nursery window with the carriage and went down to the Royal Gardens.

"Let's go to Red Licorice Lake," Berry said. "The red sugar sand on the north side of the lake is my favorite place in Candy Kingdom."

Princess Mini grinned. "Me go!"

"Yes, you go," Berry said.

At the lake, Melli spread a blanket out along the red sugar sands. The Candy Fairies sat with Princess Mini on the shore and watched the water.

"How many Sun Dips have we watched here?" Berry asked.

"I've lost count by now," Dash said. "There have been so many Sun Dips here."

"Supersweet times," Raina said.

"Do you think Princess Mini will come here to watch Sun Dip with her friends?" Cocoa asked.

"I hope she has friends like all of you," Melli said.

"Me too," Berry added.

Cocoa looked toward the Frosted Mountains. "It feels funny to be here when it's not Sun Dip."

"It feels special," Berry said. "And it's a special day, right Mini?"

Mini sat up and waved her cupcake rattle.

"She already looks like a princess," Melli said.

The friends laughed together and enjoyed the view of the Frosted Mountains.

When the five fairysitters returned to the nursery, Princess Mini was asleep in her

stroller. Prince Scoop lifted her up and placed her in her crib.

As a special treat, Princess Lolli had a Candy Fairy come to do the five fairysitter's hair for the ball. Fancy twists and lots of sugar sparkle were used. And when the fairies put on Berry's dresses, Berry stood back and admired how her friends looked.

"Sweet strawberries!" Berry exclaimed. "You look *sweet-tacular!*"

"We look great, don't we?" Raina said, gazing at her reflection in the large mirror.

"Sure as sugar," Berry said. "You are the sweetest Candy Fairies. And you wear those dresses very well."

After the last sparkle hair clips were put in and the buttons on Berry's dress were all fastened, the five friends headed down to the ballroom in Candy Castle.

The room decorations were colorful candies and lollipops. All the tables were covered in bright fruit leather cloths. The room looked—and smelled—extra sweet.

"This is going to be a grand party," Berry declared.

"Holy peppermint!" Dash exclaimed. She pointed to the stage in front of the room. "Look at the size of that sugar bowl!"

"Wow," Cocoa gasped. "That is a royally big bowl."

The golden sugar bowl was placed on a long table at the front of the room. The sugar in it was sparkling like jewels.

Soon the room started to fill up and the

ball was in full swing. Berry loved seeing how happy and proud Princess Lolli and Prince Scoop were as they greeted all the guests. Mini's royal grandparents, Queen Swirl and King Cone, and Queen Sweetie and King Crunch, were there as well as Princess Sprinkle from Cupcake Kingdom. Princess Mini looked beautiful sitting in her royal highchair on the stage. Berry smiled when she noticed that Mini was holding the fairy doll she had made for her.

Two Castle Fairies blew trumpets and the crowd quieted down. It was sugar bowl time!

"Good thing we didn't forget the sugar," Dash whispered to Berry.

"I know!" Berry exclaimed. "I am so excited for the big moment!"

Princess Lolli carried Mini over to the golden bowl. Her tiny crown sparkled. Prince Scoop stood next to Princess Lolli with a huge grin on his face. Mini reached her hands toward the sugar. There wasn't a sound in the large ballroom as everyone waited. In an instant, the plain sugar changed to chocolate.

"Mini chocolate chips!" Prince Scoop announced when he saw what was in the bowl. "That's perfect for candy *and* ice cream!" He held up the bowl for all to see.

"A sweet talent for the sweetest princess," Princess Lolli said, hugging her baby.

"She fits in just perfectly with the royal family," Berry said, watching the three happy royals.

The room was filled with cheers.

"She's a doubly sweet fairy!" Princess Lolli declared. She looked over at Berry and winked.

"Princess Mini is the perfect addition to the royal family and to Candy Kingdom," Berry said. "I can't wait to taste her chocolate and to see what she creates."

The Candy Fairies all continued to celebrate. It was a festive day in Sugar Valley for all fairies. Everyone's hearts were filled with sweet pride for the newest Candy Fairy and the Chocolate Chip Princess.